Goodnight Little Misa

This book was made especially for
Misa

Wishing you sweet dreams every night!

Written by Jennifer Dewing   Illustrated by Mary GrandPré
Edited by Maia Haag   Designed by Haag Design, Inc.

SKU: BK280   Date Printed: March 13, 2019   Manufacturer ID: 15436SC

Sail away, sweet Misa,
   on silver moonbeams,
   as the Goodnight Parade
      marches into your dreams.

As you drift over treetops, birds whistle a tune,

M I S A

and you watch your parade
by the light of the moon.

Owls step in together,
hoot-hooting in line,
as they spell out Misa
in lights on their vine.

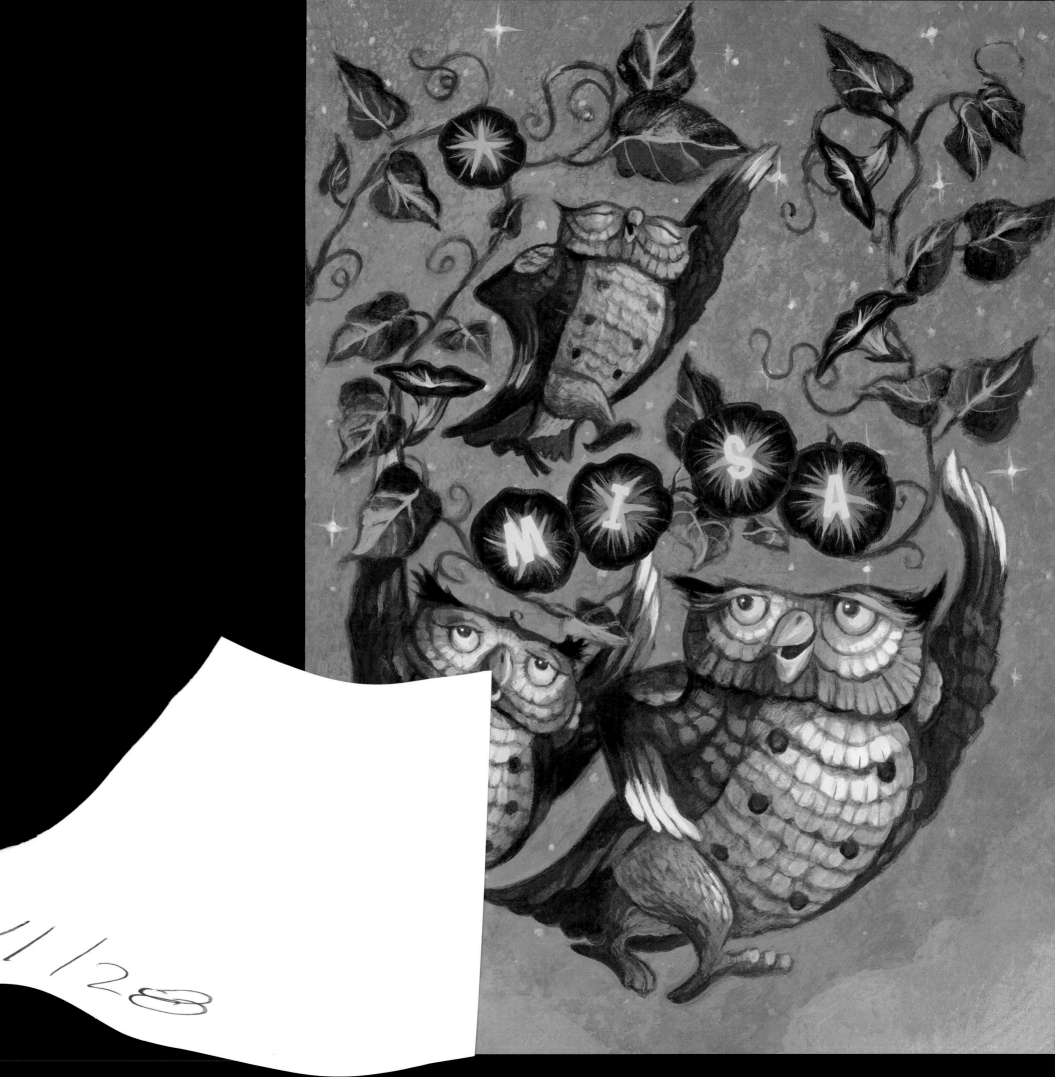

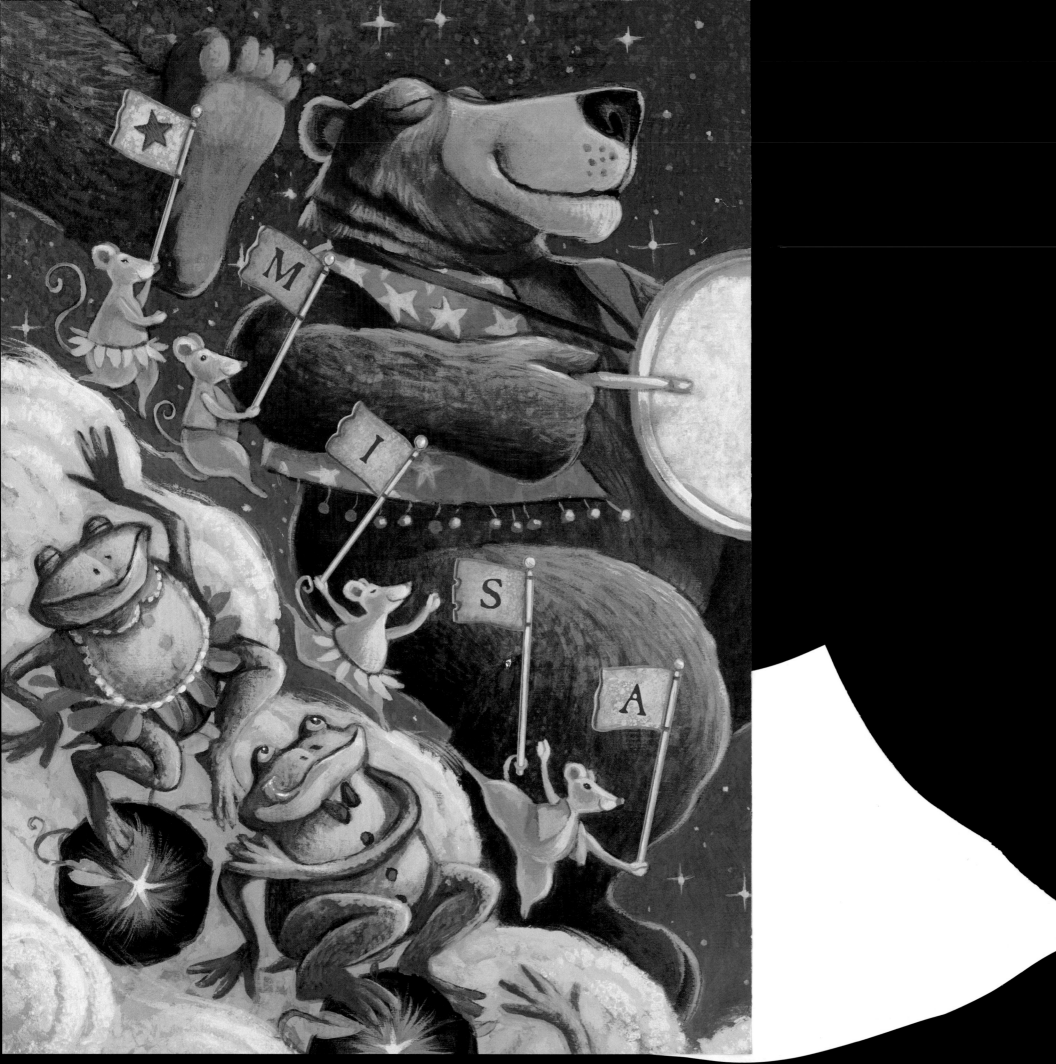

Mice twirl the flags,
while the frogs leap around.
The bears beat their drums
in a rat-tat-tat sound.

Crickets chirp loudly
and sing do-re-mi.
The sheep come a-leaping.
You count 1 2 3....

Cow comes a-jumping
high over the moon.

Cat plays his fiddle
with friends,
Dish and Spoon.

The monkeys all tumble.
The fireflies glow.

Dogs dance in a kick line
to close out the show.

Misa, your friends all sing you
a grand lullaby,
as your name is spelled out
by the stars in the sky.

Goodnight, little Misa.
Now close your sweet eyes.
Sail away on a dream cloud
across starry skies.

Goodnight Misa

PERSONALIZED CHILDREN'S BOOKS

www.iseeme.com / 1.877.744.3210 (toll free)

See all the personalized titles from I See Me! LLC:

My Very Own® Name
My Very Own® Fairy Tale
My Very Own® Pirate Tale
My Very Own® World Adventure
The Super, Incredible Big Brother
The Super, Incredible Big Sister
A-B-C What I Can Be!
The World According To Me
My Royal Birthday Adventure
A Christmas Bear for Me
A Hanukkah Bear for Me
My Very Merry Christmas
My Very Happy Birthday
Who Loves Me?
God Loves You!
My Snuggle Bunny
and more!

14505 27th Ave. North, Plymouth, MN 55447